P9-DIW-659

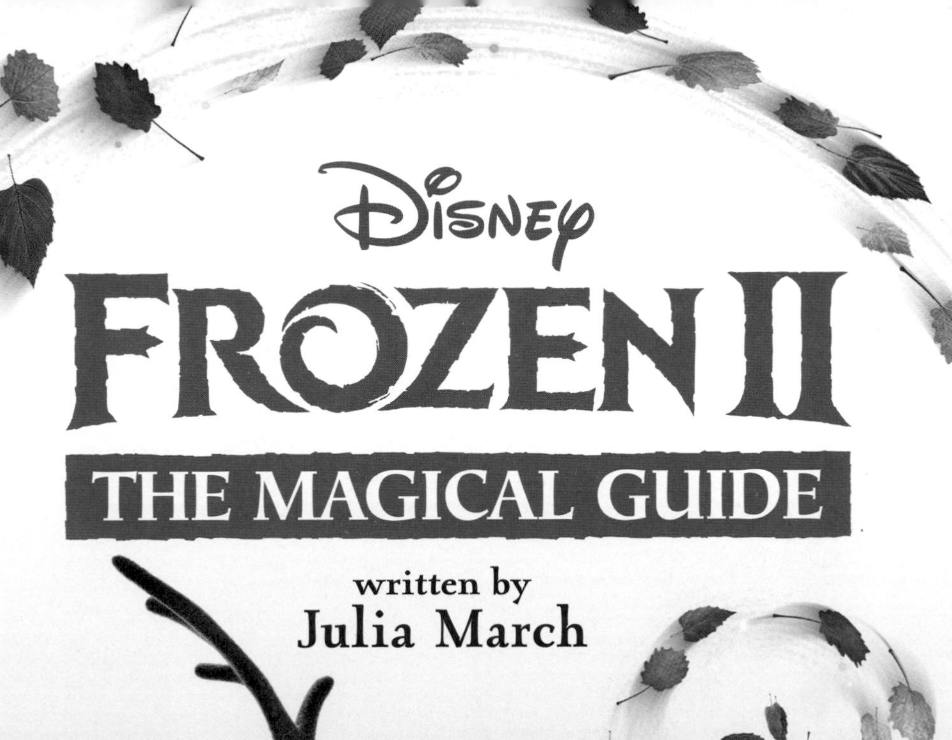

Disney

FROZEN II

THE MAGICAL GUIDE

written by
Julia March

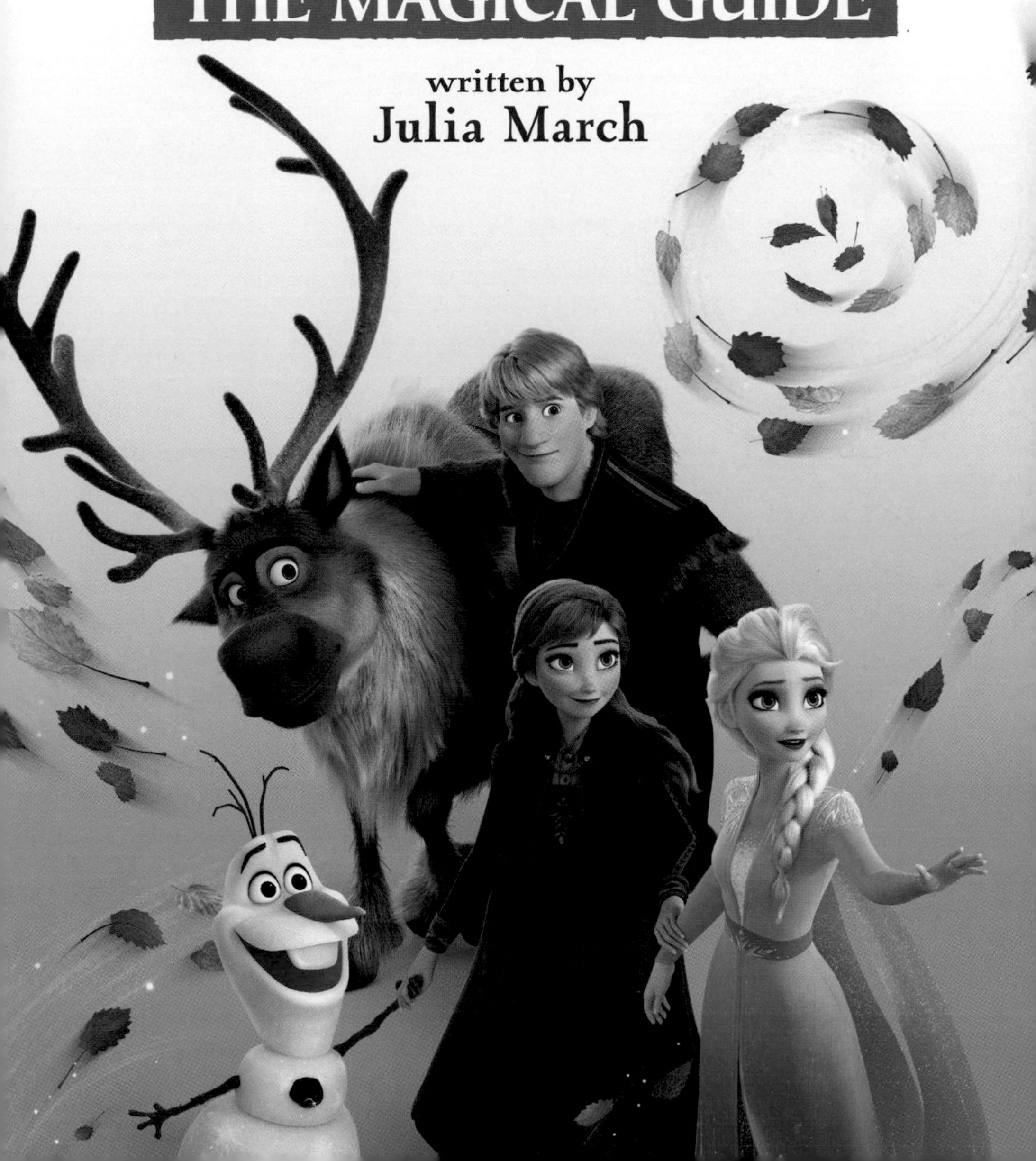

Contents

Introduction

Since Elsa returned to Arendelle three years ago, life has been good. She is very popular, the kingdom is prosperous, and the people are happy. It feels like this golden age will last forever. Nobody knows that an epic adventure is about to unfold—one that will take Elsa far away, test her magic to its limits, and put Arendelle itself in peril!

Elsa

Destiny awaits

Elsa tries hard to be the perfect queen, but royal duties are sometimes a struggle for her. She can be shy around people, and isn't a fan of the spotlight. Should she leave it all behind and follow the strange voice that keeps calling her? Maybe it can show her where her ice power comes from!

Things you need to know about Elsa:

1. She is the Queen of Arendelle.
2. She's haunted by a mysterious voice that no one else can hear.
3. She was born with a magical power that lets her control snow and ice.
4. She's afraid of hurting anyone, especially her sister Anna.

So many questions

Elsa is relieved that she doesn't have to keep her power a secret anymore. But now she's searching for answers to her own questions. And that's almost as stressful!

Why do I have this power?

I've had it for as long as I can remember, but where did it come from? How come no one in my family seems to have it?

What would my parents think of me now?

After their ship was lost at sea, I wonder whether they would be proud of the queen I've become.

Do other people have the same power?

Maybe there's magic outside of Arendelle.

Where is Ahtohallan?

My mother spoke about Ahtohallan—a secret river that's said to hold all the answers about the past. But is it real?

Should I follow the voice?

It seems to be calling for me to follow it. But where could it be leading me? Is it too dangerous?

What will happen to Anna if I go away?

Maybe someone else like that horrible Prince Hans will turn up and try to sweet-talk her into marriage!

Am I where I'm meant to be?

It feels like there's something missing for me here. Is there somewhere else where I'd make more sense?

What does it even mean to be a queen?

I'm not sure if I'm up to the challenge all by myself. But I can't let anyone know. They all count on me.

Elsa's power

Having a magic snow and ice power is one thing. Thinking up creative ways to use it is another! Here are some of Elsa's finest, frostiest moments.

Freezing rain

Moisture in the air freezes into diamond-shaped ice crystals when Elsa wields her power.

Creating ice art

Since water has memory, Elsa can use snow to recreate moments in time.

Frozen past

Elsa's magic mixes with the wind to create an ice sculpture of her father being saved from the forest.

Taming the sea

It's almost impossible to swim through a treacherous, turbulent sea—unless you can turn water into ice, like Elsa.

Foiling a fight

Elsa creates a slippery carpet of ice that has forest foes crashing to the ground. Ice work!

Anna

Sisters first

Princess Anna is Queen Elsa's younger, bubblier sister. Unlike Elsa, Anna can't help showing her feelings. She loves Elsa more than anything, but she can tell something is worrying her. Anna is desperate for her sister to confide in her. She couldn't bear it if Elsa shut her out of her life again.

Things you need to know about Anna:

1. She's fiercely protective—Anna won't have anyone criticize Elsa!
2. She rushes into situations without thinking them through.
3. Anna loves to be busy, busy, busy. She just can't sit still!
4. She cares about the people of Arendelle, and wants to help them sort out their problems.

Anna's greatest fears

Anna is normally a happy person, but lately things haven't felt quite right. Worries and fears have begun to creep into her mind. These things are all she can think about!

Something bad happening to Elsa!

I don't know what's going on, but I can tell she's really concerned about something.

Elsa shutting me out of her life again!

Why won't she talk to me about her worries?

Anna can sometimes get wrapped up in her own worries.

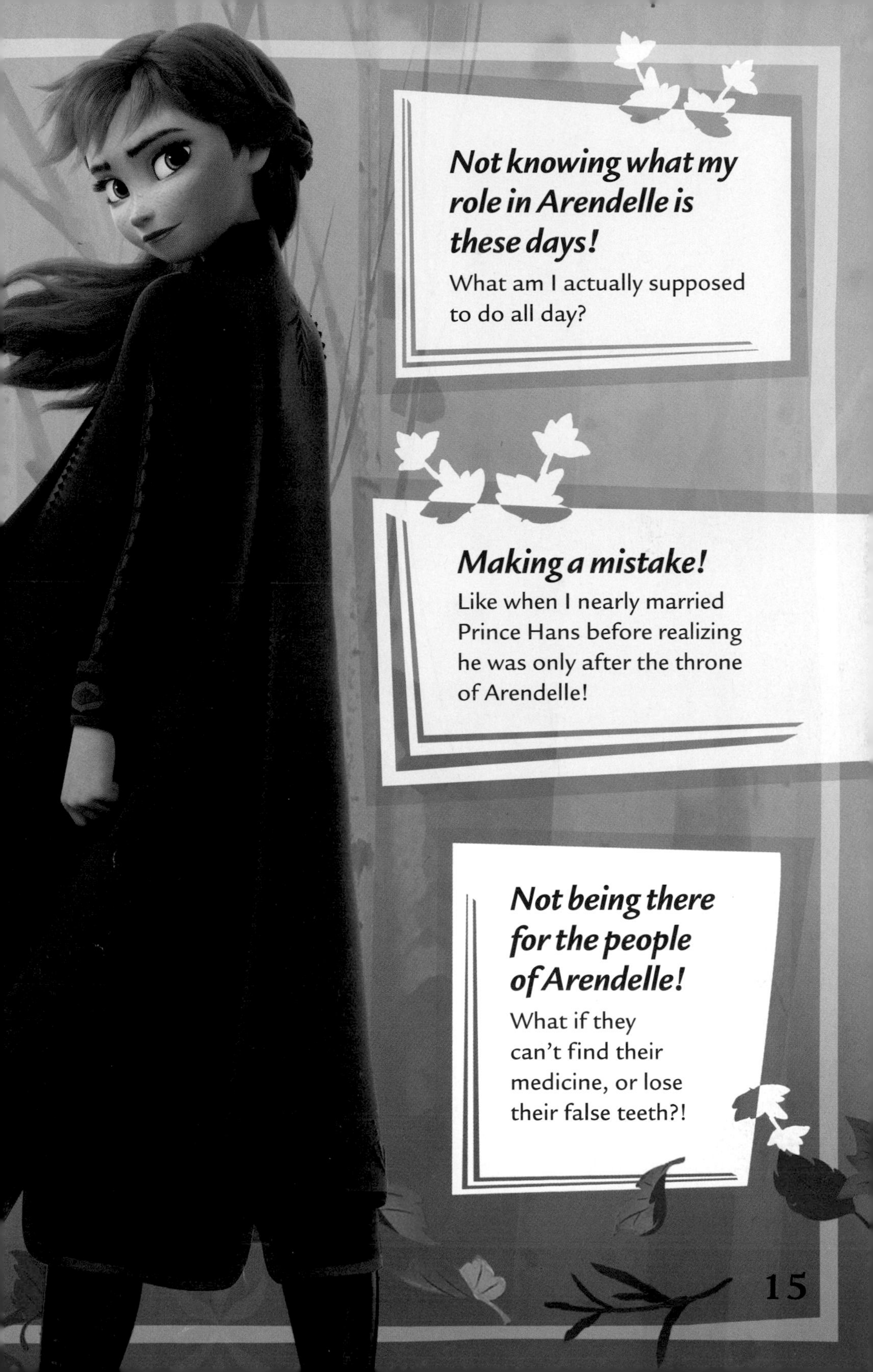

Not knowing what my role in Arendelle is these days!

What am I actually supposed to do all day?

Making a mistake!

Like when I nearly married Prince Hans before realizing he was only after the throne of Arendelle!

Not being there for the people of Arendelle!

What if they can't find their medicine, or lose their false teeth?!

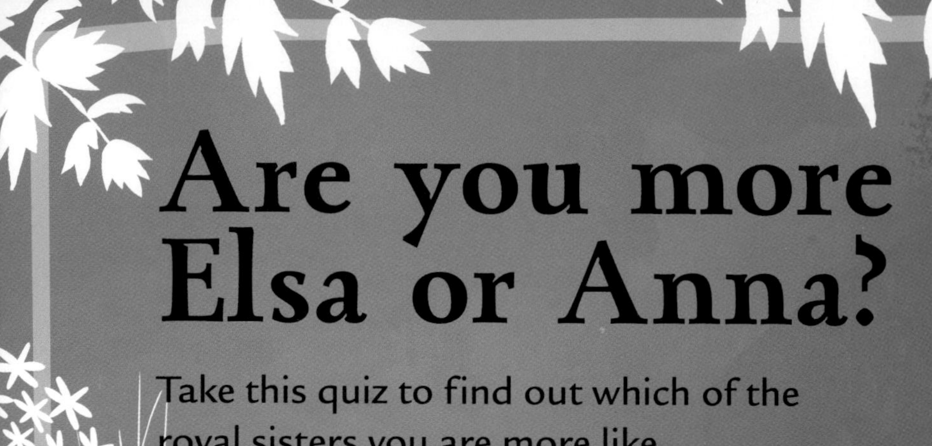

Are you more Elsa or Anna?

Take this quiz to find out which of the royal sisters you are more like.

1

Are you comfortable in the spotlight?

A. Yes! The world is my stage.

B. No! I can be a little awkward with too much attention.

2

How do you like to spend free time?

A. Hanging out and having fun

B. Being at one with nature

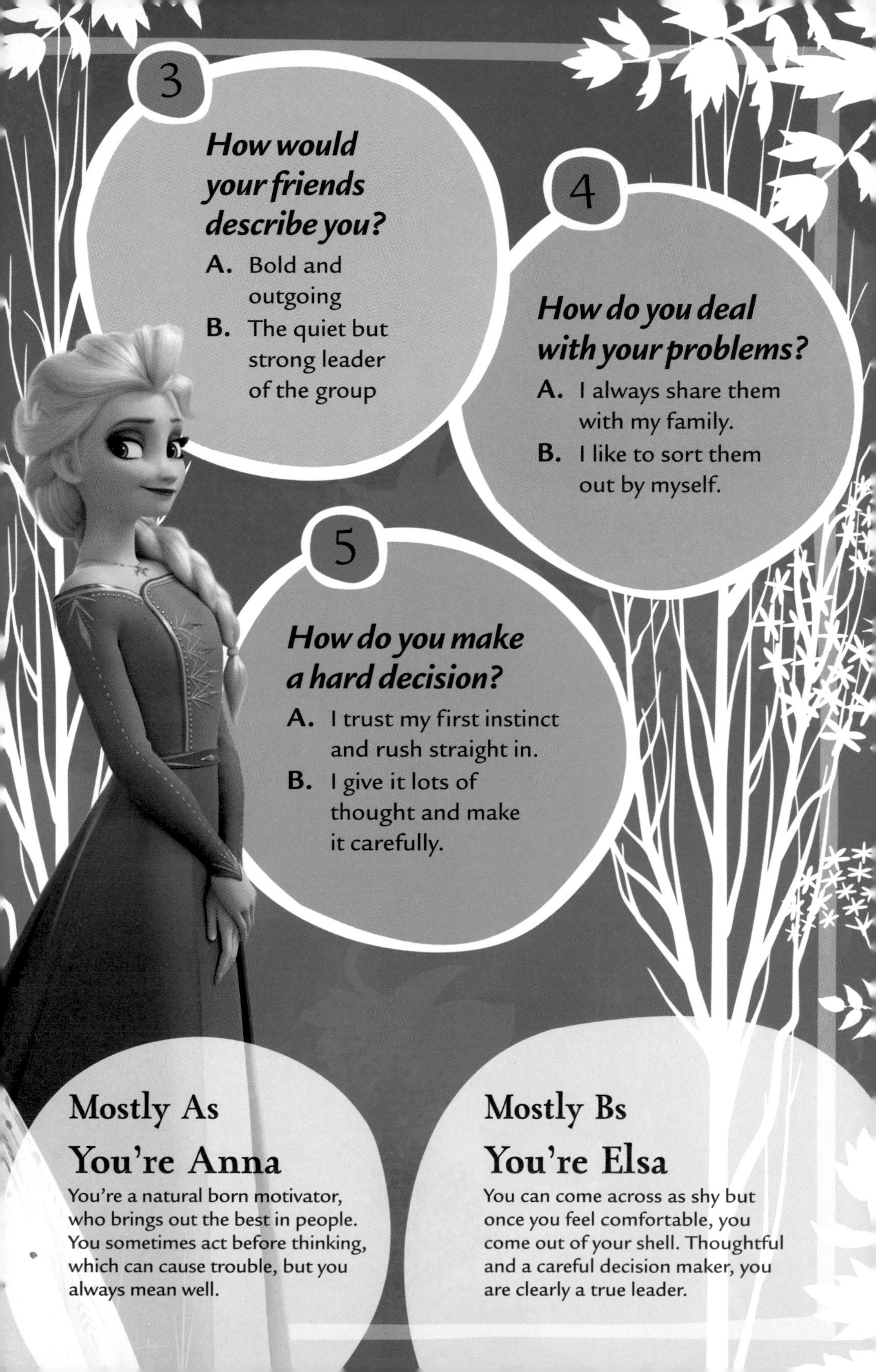

3

How would your friends describe you?

A. Bold and outgoing

B. The quiet but strong leader of the group

4

How do you deal with your problems?

A. I always share them with my family.

B. I like to sort them out by myself.

5

How do you make a hard decision?

A. I trust my first instinct and rush straight in.

B. I give it lots of thought and make it carefully.

Mostly As

You're Anna

You're a natural born motivator, who brings out the best in people. You sometimes act before thinking, which can cause trouble, but you always mean well.

Mostly Bs

You're Elsa

You can come across as shy but once you feel comfortable, you come out of your shell. Thoughtful and a careful decision maker, you are clearly a true leader.

King of charades

First he's a teapot, then he's a unicorn! Olaf can easily take the shape of any clue. His carrot is a useful prop, too!

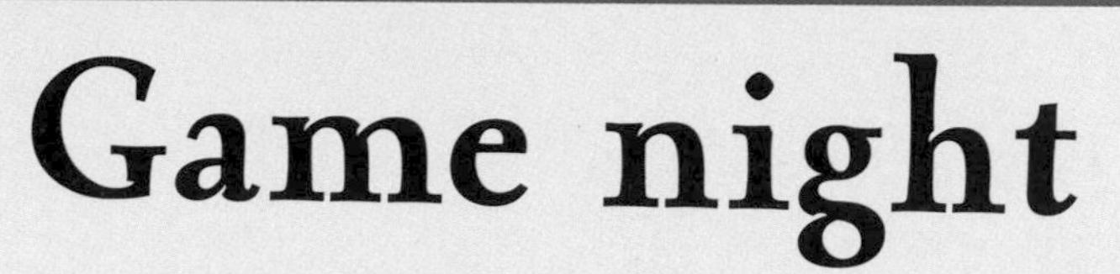

Game night

The gang love their cosy nights in together playing charades. Olaf has a big advantage, because he can rearrange his body to make clues. Kristoff is usually the best guesser. Anna can be pretty competitive too, but lately it feels like Elsa isn't focused on the game. She seems distracted somehow.

Olaf

Snowman scholar

Olaf the snowman has reached the grand old age of three, but many things about the world still don't make sense to him. He's pretty sure that they will one day—when he's older! For now, Olaf has decided to just be happy and take life as it comes. Oh, and to do as much reading as he can.

Things you need to know about Olaf:

1. Olaf has learned how to read.
2. He likes sharing interesting facts with his friends.
3. Olaf is now made from permafrost, so he doesn't have to worry about melting anymore.
4. Olaf loves his life and doesn't want anything to ever change.

Olaf's cool facts

Nowadays, this little snowman can often be found with his carrot nose in a book. He is simply thrilled by the amazing new things he has learned about the world. Olaf's friends are not quite so thrilled at hearing his endless torrent of facts when they're trying to sleep!

"Did you know that water has memory?"

"Did you know we blink four million times a day?"

"Did you know donkeys sink but mules don't?"

Did you know wombats have square poop?

Did you know gorillas burp when they are happy?

Did you know men are six times more likely than women to be struck by lightning?

"Change mocks us with her beauty."

- Olaf

What amazing facts can you find to wow your friends with?

Kristoff

Wannabe bridegroom

Twenty-three-year-old Kristoff is an outdoorsy kind of a guy. He has always relied on his reindeer, Sven, for company, but now he's head over heels in love with Anna and he's ready to settle down and start a family. He's keen to propose to Anna, but he just can't seem to find the right moment!

Things you need to know about Kristoff:

1. He was raised by mountain trolls.
2. One hour is the maximum time he can tolerate wearing a suit!
3. He is not a fan of soppy talk, but he does have a secret romantic side.
4. He's quick to help those in need—especially when reindeer are involved!

Kristoff's proposals

Kristoff keeps on trying to ask Anna to marry him. He has the love, he has the ring, and he has the words. He just doesn't seem to have the timing!

1

In the library after charades, Kristoff drops the ring and it rolls under the couch.

Doh!

2

In his wagon, on the journey to the Enchanted Forest, Elsa wakes up and accidentally interrupts the proposal.

Oops!

3

By the dam in the forest Anna thinks Kristoff is trying to warn her of danger, and runs off.

Darn!

4

Kristoff plans a Northuldra ritual at a flower-filled cove, but Anna doesn't turn up. She's gone off with Elsa.

Sigh!

5

In the forest, Kristoff finally makes it all the way through a proposal. It's almost too much for an emotional Sven to take!

Surprise!

Sven

Reindeer buddy

Wherever Kristoff goes, Sven goes too. This loyal reindeer has followed his human over hills and mountains, ice and snow, into danger and out of it. Kristoff often amuses himself by speaking Sven's thoughts. He's sure he knows what Sven is thinking. Sven knows Kristoff isn't always right!

Things you need to know about Sven:

1. When Kristoff is upset, Sven rests a comforting hoof on his back.
2. He isn't afraid of danger when it comes to saving his friends.
3. He keeps time and score for the gang's game nights.
4. He doesn't think much of Kristoff's attempts to speak for him!

Which sidekick are you?

Take the quiz to discover which of these loyal companions is most like you!

1

Would you describe yourself as a chatterbox?

A. Yes, I could talk for hours, even if nobody is listening.

B. No—I may be a deep thinker but I'm a person of few words.

2

How do you feel about hard work—pulling a wagon with four passengers, for example?

A. Um... I'd rather sit in the wagon and read a book.

B. Only four passengers? Call that hard work?

3

If your best friend is feeling upset, how do you comfort them?

A. I try to cheer them up by being funny and talking positively.

B. I stay quietly by their side, and maybe give them a gentle back rub.

4

Do you tend to just accept anything you read or hear?

A. Yes, why not? People wouldn't write or say something that wasn't true!

B. No, I only trust my own instincts and people I know well.

5

Are you curious?

A. You bet! If anything new or strange is going on, I'll be there in a heartbeat!

B. Not really. Mind you, I'm up for an adventure if it's for a good cause.

Mostly As

You're Olaf

Full of jokes and fun, you're great at making friends laugh. You're curious about the world around you and love to learn new things.

Mostly Bs

You're Sven

Quiet but confident, you are smart and don't need to be the center of attention. You are always ready to help those you love.

King Agnarr

Protective father

Agnarr was just 14 when his life changed in a day. He saw his father, King Runeard, die in a brutal forest battle, one he only escaped himself because of a mysterious savior. Agnarr came home the new King of Arendelle that night, but the echoes of that day haunted him forever.

Things you need to know about King Agnarr:

1. Agnarr met his wife-to-be, Iduna, shortly after returning home.
2. He would do anything to keep his wife and his daughters safe.
3. He warned his daughters that the past has a way of returning.
4. Agnarr learned to take the hint when Queen Iduna wanted to chat with their daughters alone!

Queen Iduna

Loving mother

Before her tragic death at sea, Elsa and Anna's mother was the Queen of Arendelle. Iduna was a warm and nurturing mother who tried to make her daughters feel safe, even if that meant hiding the past from them. In secret, she sought ways to help them, and her people, heal their world.

Things you need to know about Queen Iduna:

1. Queen Iduna didn't come from royalty. Her beginnings were far more humble.
2. She used to sing a special lullaby to Elsa and Anna.
3. When Elsa was a toddler, Iduna used to call her "little Snow."
4. Elsa and Anna treasure Iduna's scarf, which is covered with mystical symbols.

King Runeard

Royal ancestor

King Runeard of Arendelle was King Agnarr's father and Elsa and Anna's grandfather. Although quite stern, Runeard seemed to be a man of peace, and offered friendship to the neighboring Northuldra. But deep down, Runeard did not trust the Northuldra. They followed magic—something he detested.

Things you need to know about King Runeard:

1. His life's work was securing a safe and prosperous future for Arendelle.
2. He had a huge dam built that connected the Northuldra lands.
3. He had a poker face—it was hard to tell what he was really thinking.
4. King Runeard died when Agnarr was only 14.

"Always stay
one step ahead of
everyone. Your secrets
are your greatest weapon."
- Runeard

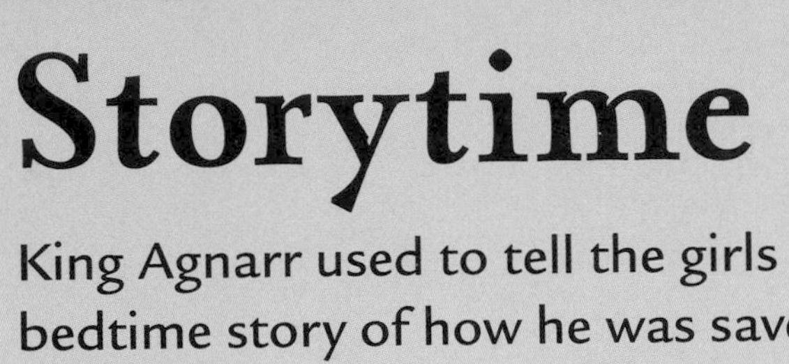

Storytime

King Agnarr used to tell the girls an epic bedtime story of how he was saved from the Enchanted Forest. The girls had so many questions... but so did Agnarr!

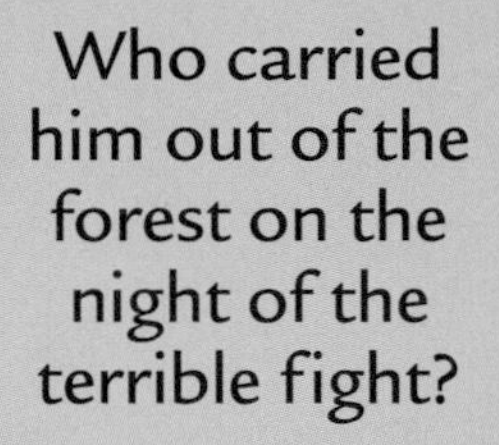

Who carried him out of the forest on the night of the terrible fight?

Why did they save him?

Is there a way through the magical mist that now encircles the forest?

Whose was the haunting voice he heard as he was being lifted up?

Agnarr doesn't know the answers to these questions, but one thing he does know:
"The past has a way of returning, and when it does, we must be prepared... for Arendelle's sake."

What happened to the Arendellian soldiers who were left in the forest, trapped by the mist?

"Now sleep,
my little
Snow."
- Queen Iduna

Magic awakens

What happens when ancient magic is suddenly awoken?

1

Elsa is unable to resist the voice that calls to her. She allows it to lead her from the castle.

2

Her magic starts to do odd things, shaping snow into strange creatures and a magical forest.

3

A shock wave shoots out, which freezes the moisture in the air into crystals. The crystals have mysterious symbols on them.

4

There's a flash of light from the north, and the crystals start crashing to the ground—heading straight for Arendelle!

5

In Arendelle, there is chaos—lanterns go out, fountains dry up, and animals' water troughs are drained.

6

A strong wind prods and pushes people out of their homes.

7

The Earth rumbles and shakes. It forces the people out of their kingdom and up onto the safer cliffs.

8

Elsa is sure this is something to do with the Enchanted Forest. Is the past returning as King Agnarr predicted?

Grand Pabbie

Troll in control

Grand Pabbie is the wise old leader of the trolls. He is the first to realize that the spirits of nature have awoken and are angry. Grand Pabbie cannot work out exactly why, but he knows that an ancient wrong must be put right—and Elsa and her friends are the only ones who can do it!

Things you need to know about Grand Pabbie:

1. Like Elsa, he can feel the spirits of nature.
2. He is trustworthy—he looks after the people of Arendelle.
3. He can move the Northern Lights in the sky with his hands.
4. He is afraid that Elsa's power might not be enough to take on the spirits.

Troll wisdom

Grand Pabbie is the only one who seems to know how to fix the chaos in Arendelle. He has some important information for Elsa.

"The spirits of nature are awake, and they are still very angry."

"Much about the past is not what it seems."

He travels by curling into a boulder and rolling himself along.

"A wrong demands resolution. Without it there is no future."
"All one can do is the next right thing."
"Be prepared– the spirits will challenge you every step of the way."

Thick cloak with warm lining
Clasp holds her cloak in place.
Elaborate shoulder details make it clear she is royalty.
Lightweight coat—Elsa doesn't feel the cold!
Embroidered decoration
Practical knee-length travel boots
Tiny pearl buttons line the back.
Gem details on the hem

Ready for adventure!

Elsa is determined to make Arendelle safe again. Her journey to put right the wrongs of the past leads her to the Enchanted Forest. Elsa and her friends will need the right clothing if they are to survive this voyage into the unknown.

Kristoff

Kristoff is used to working outdoors. His usual woolen tunic and leather boots are just perfect!

Sven

Even a reindeer can take pride in his appearance! Sven loves his new, custom-made harness.

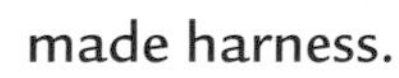

"It's magic.
I can feel it."
- Elsa

The mist

A sparkling mist surrounds the forest. When the friends try to walk through it, they bounce off. No amount of pushing or shoving will get them through. Elsa decides to try a gentler approach. She calls her friends together, and links hands with Anna. The magical mist begins to part!

Elsa runs toward the mist.

Anna can't wait to find out what is behind the magical mist.

Each monolith has
a different symbol.
The mist pushes the
group around!

Monoliths

As the sparkling forest mist parts, four huge stone monoliths are revealed. Each has a symbol on it that represents one of the elements of nature: wind, fire, water, and earth. Could they be clues for Elsa?

The Northuldra

The Northuldra are an adventurous people. They are deeply connected to their environment and the spirits of the natural world. After the Northuldra battled the Arendellians at the dam, the spirits turned against both groups. As a result, they were all trapped inside the Enchanted Forest by a magical mist.

Things you need to know about the Northuldra:

1. They are experts at hiding themselves away in the forest.
2. The Northuldra are very connected to nature.
3. They keep huge herds of reindeer.
4. The Northuldra do not trust the Arendellians at all.

Yelana

Northuldra leader

Yelana is the leader of the Northuldra. She feels deeply responsible for her people and is fiercely protective of them. Yelana is amazed when she sees what Elsa can do. She thought the Arendellians hated magic. Why would nature gift one of them with a magical power?

Things you need to know about Yelana:

1. At first, Yelana thinks Elsa's magic is all spells and sorcery.
2. She doesn't believe that her people were responsible for the terrible events at the dam.
3. She believes in listening to what nature has to say.
4. She is furious with Elsa for awakening the spirits.

Mattias

Loyal lieutenant

Mattias was King Agnarr's guard when Agnarr was a child. He had no idea what happened to the king after the day of the great battle, and is thrilled to hear that Agnarr made it out alive. Mattias firmly believes the Northuldra attacked the Arendellians at the dam, cruelly betraying their goodwill.

Things you need to know about Mattias:

1. Mattias has been mysteriously trapped in the forest for more than 30 years.
2. He has never forgotten his duty to Arendelle and the royal family.
3. He's in a portrait in Arendelle's castle library—second on the right.
4. He misses Blodget's Bakery, and all of the amazing treats they used to make.

Hard truths

When Elsa and Anna show up in the Enchanted Forest, Mattias begins to question everything he thought he knew. And some truths are very hard to swallow.

Arendellians don't do magic.

So how come Elsa is doing magic right in front of my eyes?

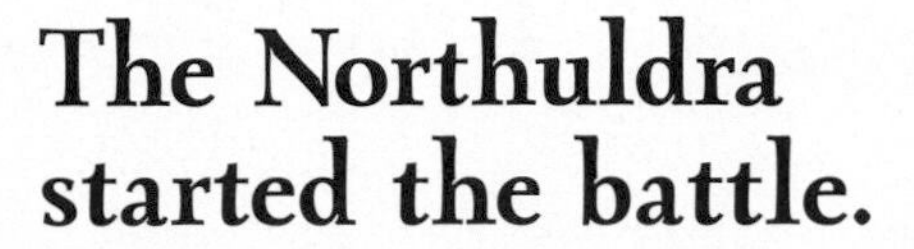

The Northuldra started the battle.

But Yelana insists that no one knows what really happened that day.

Magic is bad.

Why is Elsa using it to do good, then? She's calming the forest spirits and saving lives.

The spirits turned against the Northuldra.

Then why are the Arendellians trapped inside the Enchanted Forest, too?

Ryder Nattura

Playful dreamer

Ryder Nattura is Northuldra and he was born in the Enchanted Forest. He's heard legends about the blue skies, mountains, and plains beyond the Enchanted Forest and he longs to explore them! This breezy young man gets along with everyone and quickly befriends Elsa, Anna, Olaf, Kristoff, and Sven when they enter the forest.

Things you need to know about Ryder Nattura:

1. He hits it off with Kristoff from the get-go. They both love reindeer.
2. Whatever the situation, he has a suitable witty remark ready.
3. He shows Kristoff how to propose—Northuldra style!
4. He is willing to put past conflicts aside.

Honeymaren

Brave warrior

Like her brother, Ryder Nattura, Honeymaren is Northuldra and she was born in the Enchanted Forest. After meeting Anna and Elsa she is cautious at first, but soon accepts the Arendellian newcomers. Honeymaren bonds with Elsa after recognizing the lullaby she is singing. How come Elsa knows it?

Things you need to know about Honeymaren:

1. Honeymaren is an expert tree climber and reindeer rider.
2. She carries a staff and is always ready to defend what is hers!
3. She wears a leather belt with brass decorations.
4. She points out a fifth symbol on Queen Iduna's shawl.

Arendellian flag flies on the damaged mast.
The sisters find information inside about their parents' voyage.

Shipwreck

The sisters thought their parents' ship sank in the Southern Sea, but they find its wreck in a dry river bed in the forest. It must have sunk in the Dark Sea and washed up there. Inside are notes with Iduna's writing and a parchment map. A dotted line plots the ship's intended course... to Ahtohallan!

Wind Spirit

Mischievous but mighty

The Wind Spirit is unpredictable—it can turn from a playful breeze to a terrifying tornado in the blink of an eye! Elsa calms the whirlwind by filling it with snow to slow it down. Once Elsa has befriended the Wind Spirit it starts following her around, offering clues to Elsa's mission.

Things you need to know about the Wind Spirit:

1. It can move water and ice to replay moments from the past.
2. When it meets Olaf, it sends a blast of cold air up his backside!
3. Olaf cheekily names it "Gale."
4. Anna and Elsa wonder if their father's vision of a girl dancing in the forest was, in fact, a Northuldra girl playing with the Wind Spirit.

Fire Spirit

Hot to handle

The Fire Spirit is setting the whole forest ablaze, until Elsa catches it! She is amazed to find it is just a tiny, scared salamander. Full of compassion, Elsa coaxes it onto her hand. It burns! She scatters snowflakes, which the Fire Spirit gobbles up. As it calms down, so do the forest fires.

Things you need to know about the Fire Spirit:

1. The Fire Spirit is nicknamed "Bruni" by the group.
2. It leaves a burning trail as it runs through the forest.
3. The Fire Spirit can hear the calling voice, just like Elsa.
4. It can't speak, but it looks to the north, showing Elsa which way to go.

"I will do
all I can."
- Elsa

Water Spirit

Mysterious force

Beware the mighty Water Nokk! Those who clash with this spirit might be dragged down, down, down to a watery grave. The Water Nokk attacks Elsa in the Dark Sea, but she fights back bravely. Her courage finally wins its respect, and it allows her to continue safely to the shore.

Things you need to know about the Water Spirit:

1. The Water Nokk lurks in all types of water, not just the sea.
2. Elsa earns the Water Nokk's respect by slipping a bridle of ice over its nose.
3. Olaf is given a fright when the Water Nokk stares up at him from the bottom of a stream!
4. It fiercely guards the secrets of the Enchanted Forest!

Earth Giants

Sleepy rocks

The Earth Giants roam the north at night. By day, they sleep in the hills—unless something wakes them. When they rampage through the forest, Elsa must stop them before anyone gets hurt. She throws some magical snowflakes into the eastern skies, and the Giants lumber off after them.

Things you need to know about the Earth Giants:

1. They have enormous noses that can sniff out magic.
2. When they walk, they shake the Earth with a boom, boom, boom.
3. They stamp on foes, slam them with their fists, or throw boulders at them.
4. They can be mistaken for mountains when they are asleep.

Which nature spirit?

Read the descriptions below and see if you can work out which one suits which nature spirit.

1

This spirit hates being woken up early and throws things around when it is angry.

2

Anyone who wants to make peace with this spirit will have to pass a test to earn its respect.

3

When this spirit is startled, it tends to panic and run. It just can't keep a cool head!

4

This spirit is a flighty one! No one knows where it will pop up next, or what mood it will be in.

A
B
C
D
Answers: 1B ; 2D ; 3C ; 4A

Ice boat

Elsa won't let Anna go with her to look for Ahtohallan. It's too risky! She magics an ice boat under Anna and Olaf and launches them off in it—to safety, or so she hopes. Unfortunately, the boat goes out of control, Olaf panics, and Earth Giants line their way. Then Anna spots a waterfall up ahead...

Uh-oh! Is that the sound of rushing water ahead?

Snoozing giant beginning to stir
Anna trying to shush Olaf!

"Come on, buddy.
We can do this."
- Kristoff

Who said that?

Elsa, Anna, and their friends speak words of wisdom, fear, and love. Can you figure out who said what?

1 "*Whatever happens, remember, just do the next right thing.*"

2 "*Don't mind me. I'm just feeling clingy on account of all the danger.*"

3 "*When it comes to love I haven't had the best judgment.*"

4
I just don't want to mess things up.
5
Sven, why is love so hard?
6
When nature speaks, we listen.
7
That was magic! Did you see it?
8
The Northuldra have the most amazing way of proposing.
9
Why do lullabies always have to have some terrible warning in them?
Answers: 1. Grand Pabbie 2. Olaf 3. Anna 4. Elsa 5. Kristoff
6. Yelana 7. Mattias 8. Ryder Nattura 9. Honeymaren

Crossing the Dark Sea

Elsa stares out across the Dark Sea. Jagged rocks and towering waves stand between her and her mysterious destination of Ahtohallan. It's going to be a perilous crossing. Will her powers be enough to freeze the waves? And what unseen dangers might be lurking in that raging sea?

Elsa bravely dives into the Dark Sea.

Waves crash into the rocks

Can Elsa get past the Water Nokk?

"I know
what we
have to do to
set things
right!"
- Anna

Together

Anna and Elsa are very different from each other. But they each have their own important strengths, and together they can overcome anything!

Caring

Regal

Responsible

Natural leader

Selfless

Calm

Thoughtful

Loving
Determined
Warm
Open
Problem solving
Outgoing
Friendly

Test your knowledge

How much can you remember about what's been going on in Elsa and Anna's world?

1

Why doesn't Olaf have to worry about melting anymore?

A. Winter has returned to Arendelle for good.
B. He isn't made of snow anymore—a witch turned him into cotton candy!
C. Elsa has given him a permanent frost.

2

What did Queen Iduna call Elsa when she was a toddler?

A. Miss Frosty
B. Little Snow
C. Tiny Icicle

3

Why do Ryder Nattura and Kristoff get along so well?

A. They both love reindeer.
B. They both like singing and their voices sound great together.
C. They are both keen birdwatchers.

4

What do Elsa and Anna find in the shipwreck, along with a map?

A. A carved wooden comb belonging to their mother

B. King Agnarr's gold wedding ring

C. Notes with their mother's writing on them

5

What is Lieutenant Mattias's favorite store?

A. Cobley's Candy Store

B. Blodget's Bakery

C. Inglesby's Ice Cream Parlor

6

What does Honeymaren always carry?

A. A staff

B. A slingshot

C. A bow and arrow

7

Someone other than Elsa can hear the calling voice. Who is it?

A. The Fire Spirit

B. Yelana, the Northuldra leader

C. Grand Pabbie

Answers: 1C ; 2B ; 3A ; 4C ; 5B ; 6A ; 7A

Project Editor Lisa Stock
Project Art Editor Jessica Tapolcai
Pre-Production Producer Siu Yin Chan
Senior Producer Mary Slater
Managing Editor Sadie Smith
Managing Art Editor Vicky Short
Publisher Julie Ferris
Art Director Lisa Lanzarini
Publishing Director Simon Beecroft

First American Edition, 2019
Published in the United States by DK Publishing
1450 Broadway, Suite 801, New York, NY 10018

19 20 21 22 23 10 9 8 7 6 5 4 3 2 1
001–311513–Oct/2019

Published in Great Britain by Dorling Kindersley Limited.

A catalog record for this book is available from the Library of Congress.
ISBN: 978-1-4654-7901-3

Printed in the United States